CALENDAR CLUB MYSTERIES™

The Case of the
SNEAKY STRANGERS

by **NANCY STAR**

Illustrated by
JAMES BERNARDIN

SCHOLASTIC INC.

New York Toronto London Auckland Sydney
Mexico City New Delhi Hong Kong Buenos Aires

To Dr. Mark Milwicki and
the caring staff at Marsh Animal Hospital
—N.S.

To Ryan, Lissie and Maddie,
my three favorite snoops.
—J.B.

ISBN 0-439-67267-8

12 11 10 9 8 7 6 5 4 3 2   6 7 8 9 10 11/0

Printed in the U.S.A.
First printing, May 2006

Book design by Jennifer Rinaldi Windau

CHAPTER ONE

A NOTE!

Dottie Plum ran to the clubhouse.
She wanted to get there first.

Dottie always liked to be first. Her best
friends, Casey Calendar and Leon Spector,
didn't mind. They were used to it.

Casey and Leon got to the clubhouse a
few seconds later.

"I can't believe today is the last Sunday
the Calendar Club will meet before summer
vacation," said Dottie.

"Can you believe there are only three
more days of school?" asked Casey.

"And only four days until I go to Canada
to visit my cousin Stevie," said Leon. "I'm

glad I'm going," he added. "I just wish I could go there and stay here, too."

"I feel the same way," said Dottie. "I'm excited about our family fishing trip. But I wish you two could come along."

"What about me?" asked Casey. "Do you think I want to go to sleep-away camp without you?"

Dottie, Casey, and Leon loved summer vacation. But this summer was different. This summer they were all going away.

"And who will check the Help Box when we're not here?" asked Casey.

The Help Box sat right outside the clubhouse front door. Usually, it was empty. But sometimes there was a note inside asking for help.

"Whose turn is it to check the box today?" Casey asked.

Dottie took out her notebook. She carried it wherever she went. Inside, she kept lists. Her favorite list was of the weather.

Today, her weather list said, it is not going to thunder.

Yesterday, there had been a big storm. The thunder was very loud. The three friends went to sleep with lightning flashing overhead.

They were very relieved to wake up to a beautiful day.

Dottie flipped to the page where she kept a tally of whose turn it was to check the Help Box. "It's your turn," she told Leon.

Leon checked. "We got a note!" he said. He took it out and read it.

Dear Calendar Club,
Warren Bunn is in big trouble. He needs help. Can you meet me at Fruitvale Park at four o'clock? Sorry for anything we ever did to you.
From, Derek Fleck

"Dear Calendar Club,

Warren Bunn is in big trouble. He needs help. Can you meet me at Fruitvale Park at four o'clock? Sorry for anything we ever did to you.

From, Derek Fleck"

The three friends looked at one another.

Warren Bunn was a bully in their grade — and proud of it. Derek Fleck was his best friend. Neither of them liked the Calendar Club. But they both liked playing jokes on people.

"I don't think Warren would want our help even if he needed it," said Leon.

"It must be a joke," said Dottie.

"But what if he does need our help?" asked Casey. "What if it isn't a joke?"

"We can stop at the park and just look to see if Derek is there," said Dottie. She checked her watch. "It's three-forty-five."

"We better get going," said Leon.

They hurried to Fruitvale Park.

"Do you think Warren will be at the park, too?" Casey asked as they walked.

"I don't know," said Dottie.

"What do you think, Leon?" asked Casey.

But Leon didn't answer. He was nowhere to be seen. This was nothing new.

Leon was a collector. His favorite collection was of rocks in the shape of states. He hoped to make an entire map of the United States out of rocks someday. But sometimes Leon wandered off when he was looking for rocks.

"Leon," Casey and Dottie called together.

Leon came running from behind a tree.

"Did you find anything?" asked Casey.

Leon was about to speak, but he stopped. He pointed. Dottie and Casey looked.

A man and a woman were on the lawn of a house across the street. They wore black pants and matching black-and-white-striped shirts. The woman had binoculars.

"Why are they staring at the grass?" whispered Casey.

Suddenly, the man and the woman started to run. They ran to the end of the block. They turned the corner.

"I wonder where they're going," said Leon.

"I wonder what they were looking for in the grass," said Dottie.

"Come on," said Casey. "Let's go look."

They carefully crossed the street.

"They were staring right here," Leon said. He pointed to a patch of lawn. The grass was very short.

"It looks like someone snipped it," said Dottie.

"But why?" asked Casey.

"I don't know," said Dottie. She checked her watch. "It's four o'clock! We have to hurry if we want to meet Derek."

They ran to Fruitvale Park.

The park wasn't very big, so it didn't take long to see that Derek wasn't there.

"I guess it was a joke after all," said Dottie.

"I'll see Derek in gym tomorrow," said Leon. "And I'm going to tell him that his note wasn't very funny."

"You don't have gym tomorrow," Casey said. "Remember?"

"I remember," said Dottie. "Tomorrow is the field trip to the Tapawingo Aquarium and Animal Farm. I can't wait."

"I'll tell him on the bus," said Leon. "I'll—" He stopped talking.

A strange sound filled the air.

"What was that?" asked Casey.

"I'm not sure," said Dottie. She took

out her notebook in case anyone had any ideas.

"Didn't it sound a little bit like a barking dog?" asked Casey.

"I think it sounded more like a donkey," said Leon.

"Do you think it could have been a howling wolf?" asked Casey.

"I think we better go," said Dottie.

They didn't talk anymore as they walked. They kept listening for the strange sound. But all they heard were crickets, the hum of air conditioners, and the footsteps of joggers.

They got to Daisy Lane and sat on Dottie's front steps.

They heard the strange sound again.

"I don't know of any dog that barks like that," said Leon.

Casey looked up at the sky. "Is it going to be a full moon tonight?"

Dottie and Leon looked up at the sky, too.

"Maybe we should all go home," said Leon.

His friends agreed. They would listen from inside their own houses. Tomorrow, they'd compare what they'd heard.

CHAPTER TWO
TAPAWINGO DAY!

They met outside Casey's house the next morning.

"I didn't hear anything," Casey said. "Did you?"

"No," said Dottie and Leon together.

They listened for the strange sound as they walked to school. They looked for the strange couple. But the couple didn't appear. And everything was quiet.

It wasn't quiet at school. Everyone was excited about the field trip. And Leon was excited about talking to Derek.

The teachers directed students to board the buses.

Dottie, Casey, and Leon were assigned to the same bus.

Mr. Elder, the principal of Fruitvale Elementary School, was on their bus, too.

"Are you excited about my favorite field trip?" he asked the three friends as they got on the bus.

"Yes," said Dottie.

"Mr. Elder," said Casey. "Is Derek Fleck on this bus?"

"He will be," said Mr. Elder. "If he gets to school in time."

Leon spotted an empty seat for three. They sat down.

The bus quickly filled up. Two more teachers got on. The driver shut the door. He started the engine.

"Wait!" said Dottie. She pointed out the window. "Derek's coming."

The driver opened the door. Derek climbed on board.

Mr. Elder stood up. "You're late," he told Derek.

"I'm sorry," said Derek.

He looked down the aisle and saw Dottie, Casey, and Leon.

"Mr. Elder," said Derek. "I have a question. Warren was supposed to be my partner today. But his mom wouldn't sign his permission slip. So he has to stay in the library all day and do work while a substitute teacher watches."

"I know all about that," said Mr. Elder. "What's your question?"

"Can I be their partner?" Derek pointed to Dottie, Casey, and Leon.

"No," said Mr. Elder. "People who are late to school too many times get me as their partner."

"Okay," Derek said. "But can I at least talk to them for a minute?"

"No," said Mr. Elder. "You may sit down and buckle your seat belt."

He pointed to the seat next to him.

Derek did what he was told.

The bus left. The ride to the aquarium and animal farm took less than half an hour.

Derek spent most of the time turning around, trying to say something to Dottie, Casey, and Leon.

Mr. Elder spent most of the time telling Derek to sit still and keep his eyes facing front.

Finally, the bus stopped. Everyone got off.

"Stay with your partners," said Mr. Elder. "Derek, stay with me."

Derek looked miserable.

The teachers divided the students into groups.

Dottie, Casey, and Leon's group went to the shark park.

"Can I go with them?" Derek asked Mr. Elder. "I love sharks."

"Good," said Mr. Elder. "They have a shark in one of the touch tanks. That's where our group is going."

Derek had to stick to Mr. Elder like glue all the way through the aquarium tour.

When the tour ended, the students lined up for the animal farm. They stood in line for a long time. The line didn't move.

"Wait here," Mr. Elder told Derek. "I'm going to see what the problem is."

Derek stayed where he was.

But Dottie, Casey, and Leon got permission from their teacher to go talk to him.

"Why weren't you at Fruitvale Park yesterday?" Casey asked him.

"That note you left us wasn't funny," said Leon.

"It wasn't supposed to be funny," said

Derek. "And I was going to the park. But my mother told me I had a dentist appointment and I couldn't miss it."

"Does Warren really need our help?" Casey asked.

"Yes," Derek said. "His mother is punishing him and it's not fair."

"Is that why she didn't sign his permission slip?" asked Casey.

Derek nodded.

"He must have done something really bad," said Dottie.

"What did he do?" asked Casey.

"He wasn't lying," said Derek. "He was telling the truth."

"About what?" Casey asked.

But Derek didn't answer. Mr. Elder was on his way back toward him. And he looked mad.

Mr. Elder clapped his hands. "I need everyone's attention," he said.

They all got quiet.

"There's a problem at the animal farm," said the principal. "And it's temporarily closed."

There was a loud groan. Everyone loved the animal farm.

"We'll eat our lunch and return to school early," he added.

Another big groan went through the crowd.

But they did what they were told.

They got back to school two hours early. They wrote stories in their classrooms about what they wished they'd seen at the animal farm.

The school bell rang. Class was dismissed.

Dottie, Casey, and Leon hurried to Derek's classroom. They still wanted to ask him what had happened with Warren.

"Sorry, but Derek just left," said his teacher. "You can try the car pool line."

Dottie, Casey, and Leon hurried to the gym. That's where students waited to be picked up if they weren't going to walk home.

"I don't see him," said Dottie.

"There's his mother," said Leon. "She looks mad."

Mrs. Fleck was talking very loudly to the teacher in charge of the car pool line.

"I gave a note to Derek that said he was not supposed to walk home today," said Mrs. Fleck. "The note said I would pick up Derek and his friend Warren Bunn."

"I'm sorry, Mrs. Fleck," said the teacher. "But Derek and Warren told me they were walking today."

Casey turned to Dottie and Leon. "Do you think if we run we could catch up to Derek and Warren?"

"Let's try," said Dottie.

But they were only a block away from school when Leon stopped. "Look!"

He pointed down the block. The man and the woman in the striped shirts were running ahead of them.

The three friends watched as the couple turned the corner.

"They're going in the direction of Daisy Lane," said Dottie.

"Come on," said Casey. "Don't you think we can outrun them?"

The three friends took off, running toward home.

CHAPTER THREE

WARREN'S SIGN

They **ran fast** around the corner. But there was no sign of the man or the woman anywhere.

"There's something very strange about those two," said Dottie.

"There's something very strange about that tree," said Leon.

They walked over to a nearby tree. Big pieces of bark had come off.

"Why do you think that bark fell off?" asked Casey.

"It looks like someone picked it off," said Leon.

"Would Warren do that?" asked Casey. "Is that why he's in trouble?"

"We'll find out," said Dottie. She ran to Warren's front door. She rang the bell.

Mrs. Bunn came to the door.

"Is Warren home?" asked Casey. "Can he come to our clubhouse?"

"That's very nice of you," said Mrs. Bunn. "But Warren can't go out today."

She didn't explain why. Dottie, Casey, and Leon thought it wouldn't be polite to ask.

"Can you please tell him we stopped by?" asked Casey.

Mrs. Bunn stepped outside and looked up at one of the second-floor windows. "I think he already knows."

Dottie, Casey, and Leon looked up. Warren was standing at the window. He looked very unhappy.

"Try again tomorrow," said Mrs. Bunn.

"He might be able to come out tomorrow." She went back in the house.

The three friends looked at Warren. He was trying to tell them something. But the window was closed. They couldn't hear him.

"I think he wants us to wait," said Dottie.

Warren disappeared for a moment. He came back with a sign. He held it up in the window.

"It says *Help*," said Dottie. She copied that into her notebook.

"*Help* how?" asked Casey.

Warren got another piece of paper. He came back and held it up.

"It says *Me*," said Leon.

"*Help me* what?" Casey asked.

Warren wrote another sign. He held that one up.

"*Find*," Dottie said.

"*Help me find* what?" Casey asked.

Leon read the next sign. "*The*," he said.

"The last sign will tell us what he lost," said Dottie.

But when Warren came back and held up the last sign, his mother appeared. She took the sign away from him. She opened the window.

"Warren is not allowed to talk to his friends today," she said.

She closed the window. She pulled down the shade.

"Did you read the last sign?" asked Casey.

"No," said Dottie. "All I saw was a *B*."

"All I saw was an *R*," said Leon.

"Do you think Warren wants us to help him find something that begins with the letters *BR*?" asked Casey.

Dottie started a new list called Things that begin with BR.

"Did he lose a bracelet?" asked Casey.

"I don't think so," said Leon.

"A brother?" asked Casey.

"He doesn't have one of those," said Dottie.

They thought of as many words as they could that started with the letters *BR*.

Dottie wrote them down. She wrote brush, broom, and bridge. Then she wrote briefcase, bronze medal, and bread.

"I don't think it's any of those things," said Leon.

"Why don't we go to Derek's house and ask him?" said Casey.

Dottie and Leon agreed.

Derek lived close by. Dottie ran ahead and got there first.

Mrs. Fleck answered the door.

"Can Derek come out?" asked Casey.

"No," said Mrs. Fleck. "Derek wasn't supposed to walk home from school today. He's being punished. But I'll tell him you came by." She closed the door.

The three friends glanced up at the second-floor windows. But Derek wasn't there.

They decided to go home.

They didn't get far when a loud noise surprised them.

"What was that?" asked Casey.

"It sounded like something big fell," said Leon.

A louder noise came next.

"That sounded like thunder," said Dottie. She looked up at the sky. "But there aren't any clouds."

They turned the corner. Leon stopped.

"Look over there!" he whispered.

The man and the woman were in front of a driveway.

The woman held binoculars to her eyes.

"What are they looking for?" asked Casey.

They heard another crash. The
thundering sound came again.

The man and the woman heard it, too.
They looked surprised. They glanced
around. They saw the three friends.

"Oh, no," said the man.

"Let's go," said the woman.

They ran down the street.

"Wait!" called Dottie.

But they were gone.

"They looked at us and they ran," said
Dottie.

"They looked mad," said Leon. "But I
don't know why."

"You know what I think?" asked Casey.

Dottie and Leon nodded. They had the
same idea.

It was time to call Officer Gill.

CHAPTER FOUR

CALLING OFFICER GILL

They waited for Officer Gill in front of Casey's house.

Dottie started a new list called **Strange Sounds.** She listed: **Barking, but not like a dog. Loud crash. Thunder noise.**

Casey and Leon worked on drawing a map of Fruitvale. They noted where they'd seen the strange man and woman. They

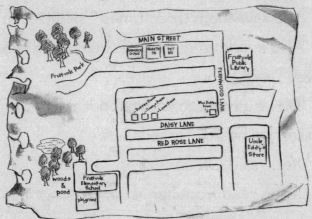

marked down every spot where they'd heard a strange sound.

Officer Gill came just as they finished. He sat down beside them.

"What's the Calendar Club investigating today?" he asked. Officer Gill took his notebook out of his back pocket.

"We saw a strange man and woman," said Leon.

"Do you want us to show you where we saw them?" asked Casey.

"We made a map," explained Leon.

"I'd like to see it," said Officer Gill.

Casey handed him the map.

"We saw them three times," said Dottie.

"And every time we saw them, they ran away," said Leon.

"Do you want to know about the strange noises we heard?" asked Casey.

"Yes," said Officer Gill.

Dottie read from her list of Strange

Sounds. Leon pointed on the map to show where they'd heard each one.

"Do you know anything about werewolves?" asked Casey.

"I don't believe in werewolves," said Officer Gill. "But even if I did, there wasn't a full moon last night. So I think we're safe from them. Is there anything else you want to report?"

"Do you want to know what the man and woman were wearing?" asked Casey.

"That would be helpful," said Officer Gill.

Dottie read from her notebook. "Black pants and black-and-white-striped shirts."

"Their shirts reminded me of something," said Leon. "But I can't think of what it is."

Casey jumped up. "I know! Don't people in jail wear black-and-white-striped shirts? Could the man and the woman be robbers who broke out of jail?"

"Anything is possible," said Officer Gill. "But I haven't heard about any jail breaks. So I don't think so. Do you remember anything else about them?"

"The woman has binoculars," said Leon.

"And they're dressed exactly alike," said Dottie.

"Those are very good clues," said Officer Gill.

He closed his notebook. "My guess is there's nothing to worry about. But I'll keep an eye out for that couple. And if you see or hear anything else unusual, let me know."

"We will," said Dottie.

Officer Gill thanked them. He got in his car and drove off.

The three friends studied the map.

"Maybe if we go back to all the places where we heard noises, we'll find another clue," said Leon.

"That's a good idea," said Dottie. "And maybe on the way we can figure out what Warren needs help finding."

"Don't you think we should follow the man and the woman to see where they keep running to?" asked Casey.

"Yes," said Leon. "But we have to find them first."

"Look over there," Casey whispered.

Dottie and Leon looked. The man and the woman were running up Mrs. List's driveway toward her backyard.

"Don't you think someone should warn Mrs. List?" asked Casey.

She didn't wait for an answer. She ran as fast as she could to Mrs. List's front door.

CHAPTER FIVE

TELLING TALES

Mrs. List came to the door right away.

Mrs. List wasn't only their neighbor. She was also a teacher at Fruitvale Elementary School. And she was always happy to have a visit from the Calendar Club.

"We just saw two people run up your driveway," Leon told her.

"It's a man and a woman in striped shirts," added Dottie.

"Do you know them?" asked Casey.

"I'm not sure," said Mrs. List. "Come on in. I'll take a look."

The three friends followed Mrs. List inside.

She went straight to the kitchen and looked out the back window.

Dottie, Casey, and Leon looked out, too.

They could see most of the backyard. But there was no one there.

Suddenly, they heard a loud crash. A thundering noise followed.

"What was that?" asked Mrs. List.

"The first noise sounded like something fell," said Dottie.

"The second noise sounded like thunder," said Leon.

"Did you ever hear thunder on a sunny day?" asked Casey.

"I'd better take a look around my yard," said Mrs. List.

She marched outside. The three friends followed her.

"Look over there," said Dottie.

She pointed to Mrs. List's fence. A section of it had fallen down into her next-door neighbor's yard.

"How did that happen?" asked Mrs. List. "It's a brand-new fence."

"That must be what the crashing sound was," said Leon.

"Do you think the man and the woman pushed the fence down and ran away?" asked Casey.

"It looks like someone pushed it down," said Dottie.

"Or some*thing*," said Leon.

Mrs. List, Dottie, Casey, and Leon went inside.

Mrs. List called Officer Gill.

The three friends went to her front window. They peered outside.

"Look," said Leon. "Emma Bunn is playing in front of her house."

"Maybe she saw where the man and the woman went," said Dottie.

"Let's ask her," said Casey.

They said goodbye to Mrs. List and ran to Emma's house.

Emma was sitting on a blanket on her front lawn. She was having a tea party with her two favorite dolls.

"Did you see anybody run by?" Casey asked her.

"No," said Emma.

Mrs. Bunn came outside. "Are you trying to see Warren again?" she asked.

"They came to see me," said Emma. "They asked if I saw anyone go by. But I didn't. I didn't see the pony, either."

"What pony?" asked Casey.

"Emma," said Mrs. Bunn, "I don't want to hear any more about that pony."

"Okay," said Emma. She picked up her dolls and went in the house.

"I didn't mean to sound so harsh," Mrs.

Bunn told the three friends. "I've just heard too many tall tales lately. Do you know what a tall tale is?"

"It's a story that isn't true," said Leon.

"That's right," said Mrs. Bunn. "I'm trying to teach Warren and Emma not to tell tall tales and lies."

"But Emma didn't say she saw a pony," said Dottie. "She said she *didn't* see a pony."

Mrs. Bunn looked like she didn't want to talk about this anymore.

"Never mind," she said. "Warren can tell you everything tomorrow."

She went back in her house.

"A pony would be big enough to break a fence, wouldn't it?" Casey asked her friends.

"I think so," said Dottie.

Leon glanced up the block. "Look, There's Mrs. Foust."

"Come on," said Casey. "Let's go ask her if she saw two people or a pony run by."

CHAPTER SIX
TRAMPLED!

Mrs. Foust stood in front of her house. She was examining her flower garden. She looked upset.

"What's wrong?" asked Casey.

"The vegetable patch in my backyard has been trampled," said Mrs. Foust. "My flowers are fine. But my vegetables are ruined."

"Can we see?" Casey asked.

"Sure," said Mrs. Foust. She led them to her backyard. She showed them her trampled garden.

"My carrots are almost all gone," said Mrs. Foust. "I wonder if it was rabbits."

"Are rabbits big enough to do that much damage?" asked Casey.

"Now that I think of it," said Mrs. Foust, "no."

"A pony is," said Leon.

"Do you think there are wild ponies in Fruitvale?" asked Mrs. Foust.

"I don't know," said Dottie. "But something big damaged Mrs. List's fence this morning."

"And Emma Bunn mentioned something about a pony," said Leon.

"Can we look around your backyard for clues?" asked Casey.

"Of course," said Mrs. Foust. "Go right ahead."

Mrs. Foust went into her house.

Dottie, Casey, and Leon searched the backyard.

"I'm not sure what we're looking for,"

said Dottie. She stepped carefully around the squashed vegetables.

"I'm not sure, either," said Leon.

He stared at the ground. Then he stopped. He bent down and picked something up. "But I think I found it anyway!"

He proudly held up a horseshoe.

"So there *was* a pony back here," said Dottie.

"Shouldn't we tell Mrs. Bunn that Warren wasn't lying?" asked Casey.

Dottie and Leon nodded.

They ran to Warren's house.

Casey knocked on the door.

Emma opened it.

"You were telling the truth," said Dottie. "There was a pony."

"I always tell the truth," said Emma. "But I didn't see the pony. Warren did. That's why he got punished."

"We don't think Warren was telling a tall tale," said Leon. "See?" He showed Emma the horseshoe.

"Mommy," Emma called. "There is a loose pony in Fruitvale."

Mrs. Bunn came to the door. "Why are you still talking about that pony?" she asked.

Leon showed Mrs. Bunn the horseshoe.

"We think Warren was telling the truth about the pony," said Dottie. "So he shouldn't be punished."

"Warren wasn't punished because he said he saw a pony," said Mrs. Bunn. "Emma, why don't you explain what happened."

"Okay," said Emma. "Warren told me there was a pony in our backyard. Then he said there was a zebra. And he said if I went out and looked with him, we might find a giraffe and ride it."

"What time was it when he told you that?" asked Mrs. Bunn.

"I can't tell time yet," admitted Emma. "But everyone else was asleep. The doors were all locked. And Warren said it was late and I'd better be quiet, or else."

Mrs. Bunn turned to the three friends. "It was three in the morning. Do you understand now?"

"Yes," said Leon. "We're sorry to bother you."

"That's all right," said Mrs. Bunn.

Dottie, Casey, and Leon walked away feeling glum.

"I guess we were wrong about why Warren was punished," said Dottie.

"Do you think we're wrong about the pony?" asked Casey.

"This horseshoe came from somewhere," said Leon.

"Mrs. List's fence didn't fall down on its own," said Dottie.

"Do you know what time it is?" Casey asked.

Dottie didn't need to look at her watch before she answered.

"Yes," she said. "It's time for the Calendar Club to go to the clubhouse and figure this out."

CHAPTER SEVEN

TRAPPED!

Dottie got to Casey's driveway first. Casey came second. Leon, like always, came last.

Leon ran over to his friends. "Look what I found on the sidewalk." He opened his hand. In his palm was a pile of sugar cubes.

He glanced ahead. "There's another one." He picked it up.

"There's one over there, too," said Dottie.

"Is that one over there?" asked Casey. She pointed.

"It's a trail," Leon said.

Leon picked up sugar cubes as they walked up the driveway.

Casey stopped when they got to her backyard.

"What happened?" she asked quietly.

She stared at the clubhouse. The door was on the ground.

"It looks like something knocked down the door," said Dottie.

"Just like Mrs. List's fence," said Leon.

"Could the pony be here?" asked Casey.

They started toward the clubhouse to get a better look.

"Wait," said Casey. She stopped.

"Be very quiet," she whispered. "And follow me."

She led them to a nearby oak tree. It had a very wide trunk. They all fit behind it without being seen.

"Did you see who's inside our clubhouse?" Casey whispered.

Dottie and Leon took a peek.

"It's them!" Leon whispered. "The strange people are in our clubhouse!"

A voice boomed out. "I thought they'd be here," he yelled. The man in the striped shirt walked out of the clubhouse. "Where did they go?"

The woman came out next.

"We must have just missed them," she said.

"They must be really spooked now," said the man. "That's just going to make things harder."

"What if we try and trap them?" the woman asked.

"Do you think they'll put up a fight?" asked the man.

"They might," said the woman. "If they're as scared as I think they are."

50

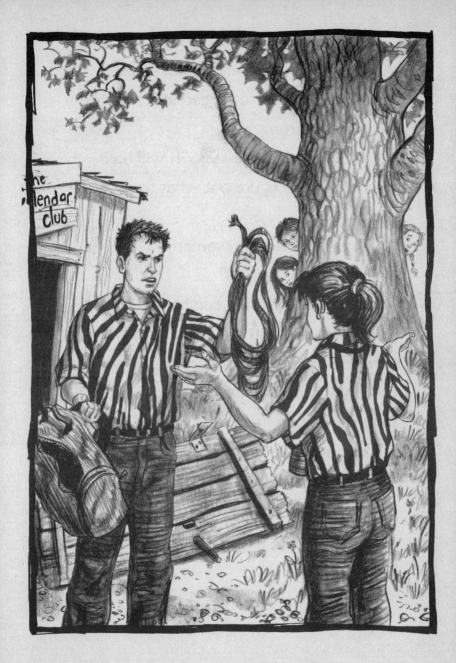

The man reached into a bag that was slung over his shoulder. He pulled out a thick white rope. He tugged at it to make sure it was strong.

"We'll use this," he said. "It will hold them while we figure out what to do with them next."

"Let's go," said the woman. "They probably didn't get far."

Dottie, Casey, and Leon had really wanted to talk to the man and the woman before. But they didn't want to talk to them now. Not after hearing about a trap. And not after seeing that rope.

They stayed perfectly still. They held their breath.

The man and the woman ran past the tree. They hurried down the driveway, and were gone.

CHAPTER EIGHT

THE HOOFBEATS OF ZEBRAS

Dottie, Casey, and Leon came out of their hiding place.

"What are they going to do to us?" asked Casey.

"I don't think they want to do anything to us," said Leon.

"Didn't you hear what they said?" asked Casey. "Didn't you see the rope?"

"They said they want to trap us," said Dottie.

"They talked about trapping," said Leon. "But I don't think they meant us." He reached into his pockets and took out some sugar cubes. "I think they're the ones who dropped these."

"Those must be for the pony," said Dottie.

"Is that what they're trying to trap?" asked Casey. "The pony?"

"From the way they were talking, it sounds like there's more than one," said Leon.

"Do you think there are two ponies?" asked Casey. "Or three?"

"I wish we could find three ponies," said Dottie.

"Maybe we can. Where would you go if you were a lost pony?" asked Casey.

"I'd go to Uncle Eddy's store," said Dottie. "He's got big bins of carrots outside his store. And I think the ponies like carrots as much as they like sugar cubes."

"You're right," said Leon. "It was probably the ponies who ate Mrs. Foust's carrots."

"What are we waiting for?" asked Casey. "Let's go."

Uncle Eddy's store was only a few blocks away.

They got there and found Uncle Eddy picking up fruit and vegetables from the ground.

"Hi," he said. "Pardon the mess." He picked up some carrots and apples and put them back in their bins.

"What happened?" asked Casey.

"I'm not sure," said Uncle Eddy. "I heard a crash. I came outside. And I found the apple and carrot bins on the ground."

He picked up another piece of carrot. "It looks like someone made this one part of their lunch."

"Do you mind if we look around?" asked Casey.

"No," said Uncle Eddy. "What are you looking for?"

Dottie, Casey, and Leon saw it at the same time.

"That," Leon said. He pointed behind Uncle Eddy.

Uncle Eddy turned around. A small pony was standing near a bin of peaches.

"Where did that pony come from?" asked Uncle Eddy.

"We're not sure," said Dottie. "But we think he might have a pony friend with him."

"Maybe his friends aren't all ponies," said Leon. He looked very pale and very surprised.

Everyone turned to see what Leon was staring at.

"A zebra!" said Dottie.

"Is it real?" asked Casey.

No one had to answer. The zebra walked over to Leon. It nuzzled his pocket.

Leon carefully reached into his pocket. He took out a sugar cube.

His friends watched, wide-eyed.

They had never seen a zebra, except in a zoo. And they had never dreamed they'd see one eating out of Leon's hand.

CHAPTER NINE

SAVING THE ANIMALS

"Where did they come from?" asked Uncle Eddy.

"We don't know," said Dottie. "But there are two people running around Fruitvale looking for them."

"We should try to find them," said Leon.

But he didn't want to move. The zebra had finished his second sugar cube. Now he was resting his head on top of Leon's head.

"Should we call Officer Gill?" asked Casey. "We could find those people faster in his car."

Uncle Eddy made the call. Officer Gill came quickly. He brought Dr. Marsh with him. She was Fruitvale's favorite veterinarian.

"I never thought I'd get a chance to catch a zebra in Fruitvale," said Dr. Marsh.

She'd brought along some rope to make into a leash. She asked Leon to help put the rope over the zebra's head. The zebra didn't seem to mind at all.

She asked Casey and Dottie to help put a rope over the pony's head. The pony didn't seem to mind, either.

Leon gave Dr. Marsh the horseshoe.

"Do you think that horseshoe might belong to the pony or the zebra?" asked Casey.

Dr. Marsh carefully checked the animals' hooves.

"It belongs to the pony," she said. "But I'm glad I checked the zebra, too. This was stuck in his hoof. It must have been very irritating."

She handed something to Leon.

His face lit up. "It's a rock," he said. "I think—" But he stopped. He pointed down the street. "It's them."

The man and the woman ran toward the zebra, smiling.

"You found them!" said the man.

"Thank you so much," said the woman.

"We were really worried," said the man. "I'm Pete Weber. This is my wife, Kathy. That's Brady, our zebra, and his friend Pie, our pony."

Pete walked over to the zebra. The zebra rested his head on Pete's shoulder.

"We run the Tapawingo Animal Farm," said Kathy. She walked over to the pony. The pony nuzzled her.

"We were just there with our school!" said Dottie.

"It was closed," said Leon.

"I'm sorry about that," said Kathy. "We

had to close the farm while we searched for Brady and Pie."

"How did they end up here?" asked Casey.

"Brady got scared during that big thunderstorm," said Pete.

"There was a lot of lightning," said Kathy.

"He accidentally broke the fence," said Pete.

"The fence made a lot of noise when it fell down. That scared him even more," said Kathy. "He's like that. Sometimes the sound of his own running scares him. He thinks it's thunder!"

"Is that what we heard?" Casey asked her friends. "Was the sound of thunder really the sound of Brady running?"

"The crashing sound was probably Brady knocking down more fences," said Leon.

"So Warren Bunn wasn't lying about seeing a zebra," said Dottie.

"I still don't understand what his signs were trying to tell us," said Leon.

"Brady starts with *BR*," said Casey. "But how would Warren know Brady's name?"

"Wait!" Leon said. "We assumed the letters *BR* were at the beginning of the word. But maybe they weren't."

"You're right," said Dottie. She spelled out loud. "Z-E-**B**-**R**-A! That's what Warren was trying to tell us—to find the zebra!"

"Sounds like you figured out a lot of things," said Officer Gill.

"But not everything," said Casey. She turned to the Webers.

"Did you snip the grass in front of a house on Appleton Road?" she asked. "Did you strip the bark off of a tree on Daisy Lane?"

"And don't forget to ask about all the sugar cubes," Leon reminded her.

"We did drop the sugar cubes to try and

get the animals to come to us," said Pete. "But Brady is responsible for cutting that grass. Zebras don't yank out grass when they eat it. They snip it with their teeth. I'm impressed you noticed that."

"And Brady also stripped the bark off the tree," said Kathy.

"Why did he do that?" asked Casey.

"One of the ways that zebras clean themselves is by rubbing against trees and rocks," Kathy explained. "Sometimes if they find a tree they really like, they rub it so much it causes the bark to fall off."

Officer Gill noticed Dottie looked worried.

"Is something wrong?" he asked.

"I was just thinking," said Dottie. "Maybe Brady ran away because he doesn't like being cooped up at the animal farm."

"You're right to worry about how animals are treated," said Pete. "There are places where animals aren't treated well at all. But our animals are very well cared for."

"We only run the farm for a few weeks a year," added Kathy. "We use it to teach children about nature. Brady really likes being the center of attention."

"What does he do the rest of the time?" Casey asked.

"He relaxes at our ranch," said Pete. "He has a lot of room to roam. Our ranch is big. It's in Tennessee."

"Tennessee!" said Leon. He reached into his pocket. "Look at the rock Dr. Marsh gave me. She found it stuck in Brady's hoof. It looks just like Tennessee!"

Kathy and Pete didn't know too much about rocks. But they knew a lot about zebras.

"Brady does not like rocks stuck in his hoof," said Kathy.

"I bet that made him even jumpier," said Pete.

"I have one more question," said Casey. "How come the pony and the zebra stayed together all this time?"

"Pie is Brady's companion," explained Pete. "Zebras often have companion animals. It's like having a best friend."

Dottie, Casey, and Leon knew a lot about that.

Dr. Marsh gave the three friends a quick lesson about zebras as she finished examining Brady and Pie.

"They look healthy," she said when she was done.

Kathy and Pete thanked her.

Leon stared at them. "I get it! You wear black-and-white-striped shirts because of the zebra!"

"That's right," said Pete. "Our uniforms

match Brady pretty well. Did you know zebras are attracted to anything with black-and-white stripes?"

"No," said Dottie. "You know so much about animals. I wish we could have visited you at the animal farm."

"Would your teacher let you come back to visit us another day?" asked Kathy.

"The principal decides that stuff," said Dottie.

"I have his number," said Officer Gill.

Pete went with Officer Gill to make the call.

Casey walked over to Uncle Eddy. "Can we borrow your instant camera to take a picture of Brady and Pie?" she asked.

"Warren Bunn got in trouble for a couple of things," said Leon. "One of them was lying."

"But he didn't lie," said Dottie. "At least not about Brady."

Uncle Eddy got his camera. He took an instant picture of the three friends with the zebra and pony.

The three friends ran to Daisy Lane with the picture.

"Warren wasn't telling a tall tale about a zebra," Dottie told Mrs. Bunn.

"There is a zebra in Fruitvale," added Leon.

Casey handed Mrs. Bunn the photograph. Mrs. Bunn looked surprised.

"They escaped from the Tapawingo Animal Farm," Leon explained.

"They got lost and ended up here," Dottie added.

"We know Warren is being punished for other things, too," said Casey. "But can he at least be done with the part of his punishment that's for lying?"

"Yes," said Mrs. Bunn. "I'll go talk to him now."

Dottie, Casey, and Leon rushed back to Uncle Eddy's store. They wanted to spend more time with their new striped friend.

But they were too late. The zebra and pony were already gone.

"Don't worry," said Uncle Eddy. "Officer Gill spoke to Mr. Elder. And your entire school is going to the Tapawingo Animal Farm the day after tomorrow. Do you know what Kathy Weber said?"

They shook their heads.

"It's going to be Tapawingo's first ever Calendar Club Fun Day," said Uncle Eddy.

Dottie, Casey, and Leon were so excited they could barely wait.

CHAPTER TEN

CALENDAR CLUB FUN DAY

It was the last day of school. Fruitvale Elementary School was strangely quiet and empty.

But the Tapawingo Animal Farm was very noisy.

Dottie, Casey, and Leon got to be first in line at the petting zoo. They also got to stand next to Brady while Kathy and Pete talked about the importance of sharing the world with animals.

After their talk, Pete and Kathy had some questions for the students.

"Does anyone know what kind of noise Brady makes?" Pete asked.

Derek raised his hand. "Trick question,"

he said. "Zebras don't make any noise."

"Good guess," said Kathy. "But they do. Does anyone know what it sounds like?"

Warren's hand shot up. "Everyone knows that," he said. "They sound like a horse. Like this."

Warren whinnied. He did a very good job of it. Derek cheered.

"Nice try," said Kathy. "But I'm afraid Brady doesn't sound like that. Brady is a plains zebra. Plains zebras don't whinny like horses. Does anyone else want to guess?"

Dottie, Casey, and Leon realized it at the same time.

"Is that the other strange sound we heard?" asked Casey.

"Like a bark," said Leon. "But not really."

"Like a donkey," said Dottie. "But not quite."

"Can you imitate it?" asked Pete.

The three friends imitated the sound they had heard.

Brady immediately made the same sound back.

Everyone cheered.

Pete announced there would be ice cream for all.

Dottie, Casey, and Leon walked around the animal farm together while they ate their cones.

They noticed a crowd standing around Warren and Derek. They walked closer and listened.

"I was the first person who saw the zebra," Warren was saying. "And I climbed on him and rode him all over town."

"They galloped over to my house," said Derek. "Then, I got on the zebra, too."

"It's really fun to ride a zebra," said Warren.

"Did you say you rode Brady?" asked Casey.

"Yes," mumbled Warren. But he didn't sound as sure of himself.

"Dr. Marsh taught us some things about zebras," said Dottie.

"Did you know zebras don't have strong backs like horses?" asked Casey.

"That's why you can't ride zebras," said Leon.

"It would really hurt their backs," said Dottie. "Unless you were a really little kid."

"Okay, I didn't really ride on him," said Warren.

"He was just joking," said Derek.

Dottie, Casey, and Leon walked away. Their classmates followed them. They had a lot of questions about zebras. And the three friends were happy to answer them.

Finally, the fun day was over. Almost

everyone slept on the bus on the way back to school.

Dottie, Casey, and Leon walked home together. They were very tired. But they were happy, too.

"I just realized something," said Dottie. "We never figured out what we're going to do about the Help Box while we're on summer vacation."

"We could put up a sign that says, *Gone Fishin'*," said Leon. "Since that's what you're going to do."

"I like that idea," said Casey. "But I have another idea. Want to hear it?"

They did. And they all decided they liked Casey's idea best.

First they got black and white paint. Then they got a big piece of wood.

They painted the wood with black-and-white stripes, like a zebra's.

The paint dried, and they printed their

message: "BE BACK SOON. GONE TO VISIT BRADY."

They nailed the sign to the Help Box.

"Did you ever wonder why summer starts so slow," said Casey, "and then goes by so fast?"

"It's a mystery," said Dottie.

"Maybe we can solve it someday," said Leon.

The three friends smiled. Maybe they could. After all, they were pretty good at solving mysteries.

The Monthly Calendar

~~~~~~ Issue Eight • Volume Eight ~~~~~~

JUNE

Publisher: Casey Calendar
Editor: Dottie Plum
Fact Checker: Leon Spector

Calendar Club's Amazing Summertime Discovery!

The big news in Fruitvale this June was the appearance of two strangers running all over town.

The other news was that Derek Fleck left a note in the Calendar Club Help Box. It said Warren Bunn needed help. But it didn't say why.

Finally, there were strange noises: a barking sound, a crashing noise, and thunder, even though the sun was shining!

Luckily, Calendar Club Members Casey Calendar, Dottie Plum, and Leon Spector were on the case. They followed a trail of sugar cubes and ended up figuring everything out. And they made a new striped friend along the way!

DOTTIE'S WEATHER BOX

This June was hotter than last June. Last June, the temperature was over 90° for six days.

This June, the temperature was over 90° for sixteen days.

How many days was the temperature over 90° in all?

ASK LEON

Do you have a question for Leon Spector? If you do, send it to him and he'll answer it for you. (Especially if it's about a state!)

Dear Leon,

Does any state have a zebra as its state animal?

Your friend,

Jungle Jim

Dear Jungle Jim,
I don't know of any state that has a zebra as its state animal. But I do know that the zebra swallowtail butterfly became the state butterfly of Tennessee in 1995. Can you guess what this butterfly has in common with a zebra? (Answer: It has black-and-white stripes!).

Your friend,
Leon